PETER AND HIS OAK

by Claude Levert – illustrated by Carme Solé Vendrell

Translated by Leland Northam

Silver Burdett Company
Morristown, N.J. and Agincourt, Ontario

Peter had a friend. It was a tree. An oak tree. His oak. It was a strong, shady tree, filled thick with leaves. They had become friends in the tree's time of greatest splendor.

Peter liked to climb up into the thickest part of the tree, into its tangle of branches and heavy, dense foliage. There, he jumped and climbed from branch to branch. Peter knew the tree from top to bottom. He grasped the leaves in handfuls, and felt them slip against the palms of his hands. He knew the smallest details of the edges of the leaves by heart.

Peter and his oak spent the spring and summer laughing and playing together. Many afternoons, Peter took a nap nestled in the coolness of the oak's tremendous umbrella of shade.

For hours he watched the squirrels scurrying all over the tree . . .

Day after day, Peter went out to see his
oak tree. One morning, while he was
running through the woods, Peter heard
some strange music. It sounded dry and sad.
He stopped running and he could no longer
hear it. But when he took another step, the
music started again! Peter looked at the
ground and realized that a huge carpet of
yellow, wrinkled leaves was making the dry
music under his feet.

Peter was startled. He looked up at a tree. He had never noticed it before, because he was always so involved with his friend, the oak. The tree he looked at frightened him. He looked at the other trees in the woods. Then he ran from one tree to another, faster and faster until he had looked at almost every one of them. They all looked like skeletons! Their leaves had fallen to the ground and only their branches were left.

Then, Peter ran to his oak tree.

"Whew!" he sighed. His tree still looked the same. Peter climbed up into the oak and felt peaceful and happy among its branches. He talked softly and tenderly to his oak. When he stopped climbing and gently began to rub the leaves, he heard a dry sound under his fingertips. When he looked he saw some maroon color just beginning to show on parts of the leaf. Peter tried hard to rub it off with his fingers, but the stain wouldn't go away. The leaf broke loose from the branch and slowly drifted to the ground.

Peter began to climb nervously throughout the tree. He inspected the oak from its lowest to its highest branches.

His tree, too, looked sick. Peter caressed it and asked how it was feeling, his voice quivering with fear.

Peter was tired out from so much climbing. He settled himself comfortably in a knot of thick branches. The sick tree lulled him to sleep as it rocked in the wind. It knew very well that Peter was afraid, but the oak couldn't comfort him. It could only cradle him gently. And its leaves continued to fall, in withered reds and yellows.

When he woke up, Peter decided that he just had to do something for his tree. The woods around him looked like a sea of black spikes sticking up from a bright yellow beach.

Every day Peter carefully inspected his oak. He looked for the weakest leaves and tied them to the branches with some thin steel wire that he had found in the garage at home.

But, in spite of all his efforts, the job was just too big for the little boy. He wet the driest leaves. He picked out the insects. He took some thick woolen strips from his house and wrapped them tenderly around the oak's trunk. The rags used for polishing the family's shoes disappeared mysteriously. His grandfather's old woolen clothes, which had been carefully stored in a trunk in the attic, were used to warm up the great tree that was shivering in the cold.

Yes, it was very cold. The sun that used to play upon the leaves no longer appeared. The days were very short and the nights much too long and cold. Now, when Peter went to visit his oak, he was able to walk across the green pond that had iced over. It was hard and shiny, and could support his light weight.

All winter long, day after day, Peter fought to save his tree.

But as much as the oak seemed to fight back, each day it lost some more leaves, which made a golden red wrapping around the base of the trunk.

The boy could no longer gather up all the leaves. Up in the tree, here and there he grasped one from the wind. He would slip and fall, and then climb some more. He wore himself out in the struggle.

He no longer felt the cold, nor did he see the snow that weighed down the leaves and made them fall. He cried with sadness, but he never stopped his work.

He thought he was losing the battle to save his friend. Often he would forget where he was and what he was doing. And every night, before he went home to bed, he snuggled up next to the dry trunk on the rags which had become hardened with ice, and tried to console the tree.

One morning, only a few withered leaves were still left on the tree. Under the faint warmth of the sun, Peter was feeling very sad as he looked over the branches again and again.

Suddenly though, he discovered something. On the top of the branches, and all around them, some little balls had appeared. They were soft to the touch and were bursting out of the bark. Scratching them a little, Peter could see tiny points sticking out. They were a faint, delicate green color.

The whole tree was covered with these little buds, and every morning they seemed to keep swelling up. They began to cover the same places where all the leaves had fallen from. Could it be another disease? No, Peter thought, it was something much too pretty to be a disease.

Peter went to look at the other trees around him. Every one of them had these tiny, downy buds on their branches!

Each day dawn came earlier and earlier, and the sun shone brightly all day long making the trees change very quickly. The silky buds swelled and swelled until they broke open and let out strange little green shapes. They were soft and woolly, and little by little they opened with the morning dew.

To the boy's amazement they reached out toward the sun and grew.

Peter soon discovered that the same toothy shapes of the old leaves had returned to his tree. He went from branch to branch, visiting all of his oak tree. He felt very happy. And then he burst out laughing. He had saved his friend! The leaves had come back, and they felt smooth and strong to his touch. Peter laughed in the sun and hugged the tree trunk next to his cheek. He unwrapped the scarf from the tree, and leaped up to throw it far away. All of a sudden he stood very still and listened. The woods were alive and singing a leafy song. Now, instead of a sad song, it was soft and pleasant like the tender, green leaves.

The birches, the beeches and the maples—all the trees had come to life again! Peter continued through the woods and once again found the long leaves of the willows, and the rough ones of the mulberry trees.

He understood none
of it. And he didn't
try to understand. He
was very contented.
He felt happy.
Everything was as he
wanted it to be. Peter
climbed up into the
tree. He got
comfortable on a low
branch of his oak,
rested his head
against the leaves,
and fell asleep.

Published in Spain by Editorial Miñón as
Pedro Y Su Roble

First published in the United States in 1985 by
Silver Burdett Company,
Morristown, N.J.

Published simultaneously in Canada by
GLC Publishers Ltd., Agincourt, Ontario

ISBN 0-382-09141-8

Library of Congress Catalog
Card Number 85-40499

Depósito Legal: M. 27782-1985
Edime, S. A. - MOSTOLES (MADRID)

Printed in Spain